THIS WALKER BOOK BELONGS TO:

Miss Eleanor Joan
Becker

Christmas 2016.

For William
P.A.

First published 1988 by Walker Books Ltd
87 Vauxhall Walk, London SE11 5HJ

Text © 1988 Pam Ayres
Illustrations © 1988 Graham Percy

This edition published 1990

Printed and bound in Italy by L.E.G.O., Vicenza

British Library Cataloguing in Publication Data
Ayres, Pam
When dad fills in the garden pond.
I. Title II. Percy, Graham
823'.914 [J]   PZ7
ISBN 0-7445-1437-1

WHEN DAD FILLS IN
THE
GARDEN POND

Written by
PAM AYRES

Illustrated by
GRAHAM PERCY

WALKER BOOKS
LONDON

Here's our pond we love so much,
It's down behind our rabbit hutch.

Mum wants Dad to fill it in,
She says it's like a litter bin.

She's fetched the spade from Daddy's shed
To make our pond a flower bed.

Mum is making quite a fuss,
But Daddy loves it just like us.

We go fishing till it's dark –
Dad says we might catch a shark.

We haven't yet, but I'm not sad,
It's nice to sit and talk to Dad.

Once when I was there with him
A frog appeared and had a swim.

We saw a fish's silver tail –
A heron and a water snail!

Ducks and moorhens visit too,

And dragonflies go dancing through.

And if I throw a little log,

Bessie gets it – clever dog.

Big or little, girl or boy,
The pond has things we all enjoy.

My family and my best friend
Frolic in the shallow end.

Without our pond there would not be
Bullrushes as tall as me.

And late at night along the brink
Badger could not come to drink.

And where else could I sail my boat
Or find out whether conkers float?

No pond would mean no fishing net;
No squirting Mum to get her wet.

No water games for us at all,

No bridge, no dam, no waterfall.

No spongy cushions made of moss,
No stepping-stones to walk across.

Nothing left to see or do —
And all our wildlife vanished too!

Now we have all thought about it,
We don't want to be without it.

Dad has put the spade away;
Our garden pond is here to stay!

MORE WALKER PAPERBACKS
For You to Enjoy

WHEN DAD CUTS DOWN THE CHESTNUT TREE
by Pam Ayres/Graham Percy

In this companion book, the advantages and disadvantages
of a chestnut tree come under a child's scrutiny.

ISBN 0-7445-1436-3 £2.99

GIANT
by Juliet and Charles Snape

Shortlisted for the Smarties Award, *Giant* is a
compelling ecological fairy tale for today.

ISBN 0-7445-1441-X £2.99

WHERE THE FOREST MEETS THE SEA
by Jeannie Baker

Winner of the Friends of the Earth Earthworm Award and
"An eloquent, visually arresting excursion into the tropical
rain forest of North Queensland." *The Independent*

ISBN 0-7445-1305-7 £3.99